All you need is LOVE

written by **John Lennon** and **Paul McCartney**

illustrated by **Marc Rosenthal**

LITTLE SIMON • An imprint of Simon & Schuster Children's Publishing Division • 1230 Avenue of the Americas, New York, New York 10020 • First Little Simon hardcover edition January 2019 • For more information or to book an event contact the Simon & Schuster Speakers Bureau at 1-866-248-3049 or visit our website at www.simonspeakers.com • Designed by Dan Potash • Manufactured in China 0219 SCP • 10 9 8 7 6 5 4 3 2 • This book has been cataloged with the Library of Congress. • ISBN 978-1-5344-2981-9 • ISBN 978-1-5344-2982-6 (eBook)

LITTLE SIMON

New York   London   Toronto   Sydney   New Delhi

Love, love, love.

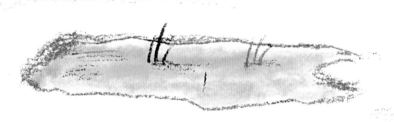

Love, love, love.

Love, love, love.

There's nothing you can do that can't be done.

Nothing you can sing that can't be sung.

Nothing you can say, but you can learn how to play the game.

There's nothing you can make that can't be made.

No one you can save that can't be saved.

Nothing you can do, but you can learn how to be you in time.

It's easy!

All you need is love.

All you need is love.

All you need is love, love. Love is all you need.

Love, love, love.

Love, love, love.

Love, love, love.

All you need is love.

All you need is love.

All you need is love, love.

Love is all you need.

There's nothing you can know that isn't known.

Nothing you can see that isn't shown.

Nowhere you can be that isn't where you're meant to be.

It's easy!

All you need is love. All you need is love.

All you need is love, love. Love is all you need.

All you need is love.

All together now!

All you need is love.

Everybody!

All you
need is love,

Love is all you need.